nasen
Helping Everyone Achieve

NASEN House, 4/5 Amber Business Village, Amber Close,
Amington, Tamworth, Staffordshire, B77 4RP

Rising Stars UK Ltd.
7 Hatchers Mews, Bermondsey Street, London SE1 3GS
www.risingstars-uk.com

Published 2011

Cover design: Burville-Riley Partnership
Illustrations: Bill Greenhead for Illustration Ltd. / iStock
Text design and typesetting: Geoff Rayner
Publisher: Gill Budgell
Publishing manager: Sasha Morton
Editorial consultants: Lorraine Petersen and Dee Reid
Editorial: Jane Wood

British Library Cataloguing in Publication Data.
A CIP record for this book is available from the British Library.

ISBN: 978-1-84680-975-0

Printed in the UK by Ashford Colour Press Ltd, Gosport, Hampshire

CONTENTS

MEET THE GANG-STARS!

Jacky

Tom

Natalie

Zeke

Aaron

?

Callum

Becca

Claire

Name:
Natalie

Special skill:
Playing, singing, dancing, acting, you name it ...

Good at:
Everything!

Not so good at:
There's nothing she's not good at, which is most annoying, especially for her brother Tom.

Other info:
Teachers think she's pale and sickly, kids think she's weird, her brother thinks she's embarrassing – and *she* thinks she's a vampire!

PROFILES

Name:
Tom

Special skill:
Plays the drums –
as loudly as possible!

Good at:
Drumming

Not so good at:
Reading

Other info:
Has a pop punk band called
Chasing Trouble. His younger sister
Natalie couldn't be more different.
He's good at the drums – and she's good
at everything else!

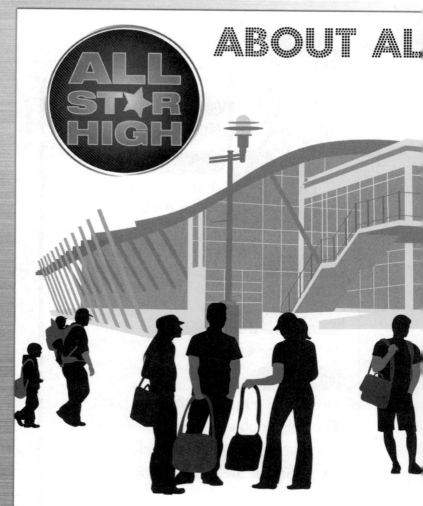

ABOUT AL

STAR HIGH

Do you want to be a star?
Then ALL STAR HIGH SCHOOL
is the place for YOU.
We will make you
a star.

Musicians,
dancers,
actors:
come see us now!

Don't miss out!

CHAPTER

There was a vampire at All Star High, but nobody screamed or ran away from it.

The vampire walked all around the school, but nobody got **goose bumps** or shivers down their spine. The vampire could dance and sing. It could even act and play instruments. What it couldn't do was scare anyone. This was because the vampire was not really a vampire. It was Natalie Caplan.

Natalie tried hard to be a vampire. She dressed in black. She put powder on her face so that she looked pale. She even stayed out of the sun because she had heard that sunlight turned vampires into dust!

Natalie was Tom Caplan's sister. Tom tried to take no notice of his little sister. She was so embarrassing. Every term, Natalie dressed up as something weird.

But being a vampire was the weirdest thing she had ever done.

Tom was a bit jealous of Natalie because she was good at everything and was in the same gang of friends as him. The Gang-Stars always helped each other. They had first met at an under-12s Music Club. It was so great to meet up again at high school that they started a gang.

One day, Tom walked into the school café and spotted his weird vampire sister. He didn't want to be seen with her, but before he could hide, she saw him. Now he would have to go over and speak to her.

Natalie sipped on her blood-red tomato juice, which she thought was the perfect colour drink for a vampire.

'What's wrong?' asked Natalie. 'You look fed up.'

'I look fed up because I am fed up,' said Tom. 'All the music practice rooms are booked, so I've got nowhere to practise my drumming and singing.'

'Of course the practice rooms are booked,' said Natalie. 'It's the Superstar **Spectacular** in a few weeks, so everyone wants to practise.'

'I didn't know that,' said Tom.

Natalie knew that the school had sent emails to everyone about the

Superstar Spectacular. There were also posters about it all over the school. She didn't ask why Tom hadn't read them. She knew the answer. Tom had trouble with reading. The letters got muddled up and he couldn't work out the words.

Natalie looked up and saw one of the posters behind Tom. She read it out loud.

ASH presents

SUPERSTAR SPECTACULAR

starring our best
singers, dancers and musicians!

choirs

orchestras

dancers

rock, pop and jazz groups

brass bands

talented soloists from
ages 12 to 18

Saturday 5th JULY at 7.00 p.m.

'I remember now,' said Tom. 'The Gang-Stars were talking about it.'

Natalie wanted to tell Tom off. He should have booked a practice room when everyone else did. But she didn't think vampires told people off. She also wanted to shrug her shoulders. But she didn't think vampires shrugged either. By the time she had worked out what to say, Tom had gone.

CHAPTER

Tom had only gone to stand in the queue at the food counter. He felt a tap on his arm. It was Natalie again.

'I've got the dance studio booked after school,' she said. 'You can come and use it too, as long as you don't make too much noise.'

'Great,' Tom said. 'Thanks, Nat.'

After school, Tom got his drum kit from Music Room B. It took him two trips to carry the drum kit to the dance studio. He opened the studio door and looked in. Natalie was dancing and singing. She was a big fan of pop music **divas**.

Tom was puzzled. When Natalie did something, she always tried hard and did it really well. This time he wasn't sure what she was doing, so he couldn't tell if she was doing it well or not. Natalie was singing a song by

her favourite pop music diva, Kira,
but she was also doing a weird, crazy
vampire dance.

When Natalie had finished dancing,
she was really red in the face. She went
and got a bottle of water out of her big
purple bag.

She saw Tom at the door. 'What did
you think of that?' she asked.

'I don't get it,' said Tom. 'I know
you're into Kira, but Kira's not into
vampires.'

'Yes, she is,' said Natalie. 'Her
latest big **hit** – 'Moonlight' – is all
about vampires. She's just done a
photo shoot as a vampire. I'm working

on my vampire dance for the Superstar Spectacular. I want it to be perfect.'

Tom wasn't so sure that the Gang-Stars would think a vampire dance would be perfect for the Superstar Spectacular. The Superstar Spectacular was special. It was the one show in the year where all the Gang-Stars could be on stage together. How would a vampire dance fit in with the rest of the Gang-Stars' talents?

Natalie helped Tom to carry his drum kit into the dance studio.

'Have you told the rest of the gang about your vampire dance?' asked Tom.

'Of course not,' said Natalie. 'I might

still change my mind about the song.'

'And about being a vampire?' asked Tom.

'Don't be silly,' said Natalie. 'Everyone knows I love being a vampire. I'm not going to change my mind about that!'

Tom set up his drum kit at the back of the dance studio. He knew he wouldn't get much practice done. Natalie wanted him to keep quiet, so all he could do was sing very quietly and make sure his drum sticks hit the drums softly. The only time he could make a noise was when Natalie stopped dancing and had a drink of water. Tom needed Natalie to stop dancing for longer so that he could have more time to practise. When a few students came in to watch Natalie practising, Tom had a great idea.

The next time that Natalie stopped dancing, he called her over.

'You're being rude to your fans,' he said, pointing to the students. 'You should go over and say hello.'

'Vampires don't say hello to anyone,' said Natalie.

Tom tried to think of another idea but he didn't need to. Someone else was about to solve his problem. A boy with spiky red hair moon-walked up to them.

'Your vampire dance is amazing,' he

said to Natalie. 'I've just filmed it. Can I put it on the internet?'

Natalie was very pleased. She liked watching online video clips. It would be even better to watch a clip of herself.

'Can I see it first?' she asked.

'Sure, come and watch it now,' said the boy. 'Then if you don't like it, we can do it again.'

'Good idea,' said Natalie. She went off to watch the film with the boy and the other students.

Tom was happy. Now he could practise playing his drums without stopping for Natalie's dancing. He played his drums and sang his song

all the way through. Much too soon,
Natalie was back again.

'Who was that guy who filmed you?'
asked Tom. 'I thought I knew everyone.'

'I don't know,' said Natalie. 'But he
likes vampires.'

Two girls came into the room. 'It's our
turn to use the dance studio,' one of
them said.

Natalie helped Tom to carry the
drum kit out of the studio and back to
Music Room B. Then she went back to
get her big purple bag. She never went
anywhere without it. It was always
full of weird stage props such as fake
animals, candles and masks. The Gang-

Stars called it Nat's Bag of Tricks!

'I mustn't forget this!' she said to Tom. 'I might need it!'

Tom couldn't think why she would need fake animals, candles and masks, but that was just like Natalie: weird.

CHAPTER

A few days later Natalie went looking
for her big brother. She was very
excited.

'I can't wait to tell Tom my news!'
she thought.

She found him by the lockers.
Natalie was hopping up and down
with excitement. She knew vampires
shouldn't hop and get excited, but this
time she didn't care.

'Look!' she said, holding up her
smart phone. 'I'm on the internet,
singing Kira's song and doing my
vampire dance.'

Tom wasn't interested. 'I know. I
was with you when that kid filmed it,
remember?'

'Look again,' said Natalie. 'My clip is
really popular.'

'How do you know that?' asked Tom.

'Because thousands of people

have seen it on the internet,' Natalie said. 'It's everywhere! And I mean EVERYWHERE!'

'You mean it's gone **viral**?' asked Tom. He was really excited and surprised now. If Natalie's clip had gone viral, lots of people would pass it on to their friends. It could even end up on a music producer's desk. He had to admit it, Natalie could become a **celebrity**.

Natalie squealed. 'Yes! It's an internet hit and I'm a superstar!'

Tom had an exciting thought. He had been drumming in the dance studio when Natalie was being filmed, so he might be in the video clip too, and everyone would see him playing. They wouldn't hear him, but he knew his way of drumming would look fantastic. Maybe he would be a superstar too, just like Natalie.

He grabbed Natalie's phone to see if he was in the clip. He could not believe it. 'I'm not in it,' he said. Tom watched the clip again. He was very disappointed. All he could see was Natalie doing her vampire dance.

Natalie's phone buzzed. She grabbed it back from Tom.

'Here, give it to me Tom. I have to go to class in a minute.' She heard a woman's voice on the phone.

'Hello,' said the voice. 'This is Kira.'

'What?' shrieked Natalie. 'No, it can't be!'

'Yes, it can,' said Kira. 'Hello, vampire Natalie, who is so famous all over the internet.'

Natalie was shaking so much that she could hardly hold her phone.

'Hello, Kira,' she stammered. 'Why are you calling me?'

'I've just seen the clip of you singing and dancing to my song,' said Kira. 'I love it.'

'Thank you,' said Natalie, who was still **tongue-tied**.

Kira had some exciting news. 'I'm

doing a concert in London in July,' she said. 'Would you like to sing and dance with me at the concert?'

'Of course I would!' said Natalie. 'I can't believe it! Can I tell my friends?'

'You can tell anyone you like,' said Kira. 'I'll put the news on my website. Keep Saturday 5th July free. That's the day of my concert. It starts at 8.00 p.m.'

'Saturday 5th July,' said Natalie. 'Yes, I'll keep it free. Bye, Kira.'

'Hey, isn't that the same day as our Spectacular?' asked Tom.

'Oh, yeah. But I can't do the Spectacular now. I'll be performing with Kira,' said Natalie.

Tom felt upset. 'So you're going to ditch the Gang-Stars?' he asked.

'Hello!' said Natalie. 'Did you hear what I said? Kira wants *me* to perform with *her*. I'm not going to miss a chance like that for a school show!'

Tom tried to make Natalie feel bad. 'The Spectacular is the only time all the Gang-Stars get to be on stage together,' he said.

But Natalie wasn't going to change her mind. She was going to be the next superstar and she was going to enjoy being famous.

By Friday, Natalie's video had more than a million **hits**. Everyone wanted to know her but Tom was not happy. The Gang-Stars weren't happy either. They wanted to perform together as a group for the Spectacular. Natalie was one of the gang. It wouldn't be as much fun without her.

CHAPTER

On Saturday 5th July, Natalie and Tom
stood by the front gates of the school.
Natalie was waiting for her cab to take
her to Kira's concert. She looked scary
in her vampire make-up and costume.

Natalie clutched her big purple bag.
She never went anywhere without it,
even when she was going to meet Kira!

'I'm sorry I can't be in the Spectacular,
Tom,' said Natalie. Tom wished her luck
and went inside to get ready to go on
stage with the Gang-Stars. Ten minutes
later a cab pulled up by the school gates.
Just as she was getting into the cab,
Natalie's phone rang. It was Kira.

'Sorry, vampire Natalie,' Kira said.
'It's bad news. I've had to cancel my
concert. There is a bad storm here in
Paris and my flight has been cancelled
so I just can't get there.'

Natalie was very disappointed. She

had been so excited about performing on stage with Kira. Now she was all dressed up as a vampire with nowhere to go.

'Maybe I can still be in the Spectacular,' she thought. 'I'm sure the Gang-Stars will let me.'

Natalie ran into the performance hall. The Gang-Stars were playing on stage but things didn't look good. There was no '**wow' factor** and the audience seemed bored. Some people were even talking.

Suddenly the power went out and the hall went dark! Nothing was working on stage either: no electric

guitars, no **amplifiers**, no microphones.
Nothing. What could the Gang-Stars
do without power? The Spectacular
was going to be a disaster and it was
happening when the Gang-Stars were
on stage.

Nobody knew what to do, but
Natalie had a brilliant idea. She
reached into her bag, pulled out a
candle and lit it. A gasp went through
the audience as they saw a vampire
in the flickering light, making her way
to the stage. She looked amazing, and
very, very spooky.

Natalie called out to the audience in
her loudest and scariest voice.

'Welcome to the Gang-Stars' Fright Fest!' she cackled.

The audience made scary noises and whistled and clapped.

'Tom, do a bit of scary drumming!' she whispered.

Tom began to drum a heart-thumping beat while Natalie lit a row of candles along the stage. 'Follow me!' she whispered to the others. 'Let's do Kira's song, 'Moonlight'!'

Natalie began to sing Kira's vampire song in her spookiest voice. Some of the Gang-Stars helped by playing their instruments, which sounded weird and spooky without any power. The others helped by calling out some of the words to the song in spooky voices. Tom kept the scary drum beat going. Then Natalie did her weird, crazy vampire dance, while the audience started to sing along to the song.

At last they finished the song and the audience cheered loudly. Just then, the power came back on.

Natalie was disappointed. So was the audience.

'Gang-Stars. Gang-Stars,' they chanted. 'More! More! More!'

The Gang-Stars crowded around Natalie. 'That was great,' they said. 'You really are a superstar!'

'You make a great vampire, too,' said Tom.

Natalie shrugged. 'Oh, I don't know. I'm bored with vampires. It's time for a change. I think I might become a drummer like you!'

'Now that is weird!' laughed Tom.

GLOSSARY

amplifier – a piece of equipment that makes sounds louder

celebrity – a famous person

diva – a female star performer or someone with a big ego

goose bumps – bumps you get on your skin when you are cold or afraid

hit – a hit song is a very popular song; hits on a website means the total number of times that the website has been visited and looked at

photo shoot – when a photographer takes a set of photographs for a magazine or for publicity

smart phone – a phone that can connect to the internet and play music and video clips

spectacular – something that is amazing to see

tongue-tied – so surprised or confused that you can't speak

viral – something that spreads quickly on the internet and reaches many people by being passed from person to person, just like a virus

'wow' factor – something special that makes you want to say 'wow!'

QUIZ

1 Why did Natalie put powder on her face?

2 What red drink did Natalie like?

3 What date is the Superstar Spectacular?

4 Where did Natalie and Tom go to do their practice?

5 Who was Natalie's favourite pop music diva?

6 What did the Gang-Stars call Natalie's big purple bag?

7 What did Kira ask Natalie to do?

8 How many hits did Natalie's video clip have by Friday?

9 Why was Kira's concert cancelled?

10 What song did Natalie and the Gang-Stars sing in the Spectacular?

ANSWERS

1 To look pale.

2 Tomato juice

3 Saturday 5th July

4 The dance studio.

5 Kira

6 Nat's Bag of Tricks

7 To be in Kira's concert with her.

8 More than a million.

9 Because Kira couldn't get to the concert. Her flight from Paris had been cancelled because of a storm.

10 Kira's song 'Moonlight'.

ABOUT THE AUTHOR

Helen Chapman is an Australian author of eighty books who has been published in the United Kingdom, the U.S.A, New Zealand and Australia. She has travelled extensively and lived in America and England and is currently living in Australia.

For further information on Helen and her books visit: www.helenchapman.com

Helen has a special friend Rose Inserra who knows what her contribution has been to the ASH series and who can never be sufficiently thanked for it.

The All Star High books are available from most booksellers. For more information or to order, please call Rising Stars on 0800 091 1602 or visit www.risingstars-uk.com